N.Y. Riverhead

Celebration of the 100th Anniversary

of the organization of the town of Riverhead, Suffolk County, N.Y. - Vol. 1

N.Y. Riverhead

Celebration of the 100th Anniversary
of the organization of the town of Riverhead, Suffolk County, N.Y. - Vol. 1

ISBN/EAN: 9783337237660

Printed in Europe, USA, Canada, Australia, Japan

Cover: Foto ©Andreas Hilbeck / pixelio.de

More available books at **www.hansebooks.com**

CELEBRATION

OF THE

100TH ANNIVERSARY

OF THE

ORGANIZATION OF THE TOWN OF RIVERHEAD, SUFFOLK COUNTY, N. Y.,

AT

RIVERHEAD,

JULY 4, 1892.

Printed by Resolution adopted at Annual
Town Meeting, April 4th, 1893.

NEW YORK:
THE REPUBLIC PRESS.
1894.

Riverhead's Centennial.

At the annual Town Meeting of the Town of Riverhead, N. Y., held at the Town Hall, Tuesday, April 5, 1892, it was on motion adopted, that the town celebrate, on July 4, 1892, the 100th anniversary of the organization of the town, and the Supervisor was empowered to appoint a committee to carry out the same; and in pursuance of this motion the following notice was forwarded by Supervisor George F. Homan to the following named gentlemen: Nat. W. Foster, D. Henry Brown, Jonas Fishel, Orlando O. Wells, J. Henry Perkins, Frank H. Hill, Elijah Griswold, George F. Homan, Timothy M. Griffing, James H. Tuthill, Charles M. Blydenburgh, Oliver A. Terry, Benjamin F. Howell, William C. Ostrander, J. Martin Wagner, Alonzo P. Terry, George H. Skidmore, Joseph M. Belford, John Bagshaw.

RIVERHEAD, N. Y., April —, 1892.

DEAR SIR:—At our last Town Meeting, a resolution was presented, and unanimously adopted as follows:

That Riverhead Town celebrate the 100th anniversary of its formation on the 4th day of July next, and the Supervisor of the town was empowered to appoint a committee to carry out the same. In accordance with that resolution, and being desirous of the aid of our prominent citizens, and particularly the old residents of Riverhead Town, I have appointed you a member of such committee, and respectfully request your kind assistance toward making the celebration a success. Kindly attend at a meeting to be held May 5, 1892, at 7:30 P. M., in the Town Hall.

Yours respectfully,

GEO. F. HOMAN,

Supervisor.

The meeting was held pursuant to the foregoing, and fifteen of the gentlemen attended. The Supervisor briefly stated the object therefor. Jonas Fishel was selected Chairman, and Town Clerk John Bagshaw Secretary.

Remarks were made by several gentlemen as to their views in order to make the celebration a success, which terminated in several motions being adopted, making the following persons members of the respective committees, viz.:

Historical and other Addresses,

JAMES H. TUTHILL,   TIMOTHY M. GRIFFING.

Parade,

OLIVER A. TERRY,   J. MARTIN WAGNER,
GEORGE F. HOMAN.

Finance,

JONAS FISHEL,	DANIEL R. YOUNG,
TIMOTHY M. GRIFFING,	EDWARD HAWKINS,
WILLIAM C. OSTRANDER,	ARTHUR H. TUTHILL,
NAT. W. FOSTER,	ZACHARIAH HALLOCK,
ELIJAH GRISWOLD,	SIMEON S. HAWKINS,
EDMUND F. TUTHILL,	GEORGE L. WELLS,
D. HENRY BROWN,	ALONZO M. ROBINSON,
J. HENRY PERKINS,	ALBERT B. YOUNG,
ROBERT GOSMAN, JR.,	MERRITT H. SMITH,
ALBERT S. TUTHILL,	SEPTER LUCE.

Fireworks,

ORLANDO O. WELLS,   FRANK H. HILL,
CHARLES M. BLYDENBURGH.

Music,

ALONZO P. TERRY.

At later meetings Dr. Henry P. Terry was selected Treasurer; Messrs. Homan, Wells, Tuthill and Foster were appointed Reception Committee: Messrs. Homan, Tuthill and Griffing elected Invitation Committee; J. Henry Perkins, Auditor; and Nat. W. Foster appointed to preside over the meeting, and Miss Minerva Mitchell was selected to read the Declaration of Independance. The Committee on Addresses reported that they had secured ex-County Clerk Orville B. Ackerly, formerly of Riverhead, and Prof. Joseph M. Belford, of Riverhead, for the occasion.

In addition to the numerous meetings of the General and other committees, a public meeting was called and held and finally the arrangements were considered completed and sufficient money raised to carry out successfully the celebration.

Invitations were sent out inviting the presence of Wilmot M. Smith, County Judge; Benjamin H. Reeve, District Attorney; all the County Supervisors, Hon. Henry P. Hedges, Wm. S. Pelletreau, Rev. Dr. Epher Whitaker, Richard M. Bayles, the President and Secretary of the Long Island Historical Society, George R. Howell, State Assistant Librarian; Prof. Eben N. Horsford and Charles B. Moore, Esq.

The day arrived (the weather was all that could be desired) and was practically given over to the affair in hand, most of the stores and business places being closed. Early in the morning the village was astir and soon wore a gala-day appearance, residences and business places being handsomely decorated with patriotic emblems and flags.

The parade formed on Main Street near the railroad at 10 A. M., and moved west to Osborn Avenue, up Osborn Avenue to Court Street, through Court to Griffing Avenue, up Griffing to Lincoln Avenue, through Lincoln to Roanoke Avenue, down Roanoke to Second Street, through Second to East Street, down East to First Street, through First to Roanoke, up Roanoke to Second, through Second to Griffing Avenue, down Griffing to Main Street, east along Main and disbanded at Bridge Street. At the head was Benjamin T. Davis, Grand Marshal. Then came the Greenport Brass Band, Leader Geehring, making a fine appearance in their handsome uni-

5

forms, and pleasing all by their excellent music. Following was Henry A. Barnum Post, G. A. R., Commander Thomas Britton; then O. O. Howard Camp, Sons of Veterans, William C. Britton, Commander; Chief Oliver A. Terry of the Fire Department, Red Bird Engine Company No. 1, Assistant Foreman Magee in charge, with machine; Washington Company No. 2, Foreman James L. Millard; the portly forms of County Treasurer Perkins and Horatio F. Buxton at the head; and steamer; the engine of Rough and Ready Company No. 3 (members not in line, many being in the march in other capacities), Quickstep Hook and Ladder Company No. 4, and truck, and a company of youngsters dragging the first engine owned in Riverhead. The apparatus were all gayly trimmed.

The Riverhead Brass Band followed, Leader Hill, playing lively selections in good style; then several young men on horseback, carriage containing Supervisor Homan, Town Clerk Bagshaw, County Clerk Fanning, Sheriff Darling, and ex-Sheriff Cooper; carriage containing Judge Tuthill, chairman of Reception Committee, Rev. Mr. Noble, of Greenport, J. M. Wagner and N. W. Foster; aged sleigh in which were seated Mrs. Everett Terry and Misses Fannie Terry, Mary Sayre and Lina Foster, dressed in old-time styles, with Fred. Reisdorph, representing "Uncle Sam," as driver; two box wagons filled with children; a wagon—Arthur H. Tuthill, of Jamesport, in ancient garb, driving—in which were seated two young ladies in costumes of many years agone, busily working a spinning wheel; citizens of the town in wagons. The parade was a creditable affair and was heartily applauded along the route.

The public meeting was held in Riverhead Hall at 2 o'clock. The room was crowded. Upon the platform sat many of the town's representative men. Nat. W. Foster presided. The exercises were opened with prayer by Rev. Mr. Chalmers of the village Congregational Church. A choir of about thirty local singers, with Sidney H. Ritch as chorister and Prof. A. M. Tyte at the organ, excellently rendered a selection. Secretary Bagshaw read the following letters of acceptance and regret:

PATCHOGUE, N. Y., June 28, 1892.
JOHN BAGSHAW, Esq.:

DEAR SIR:—I regret that previous engagements will prevent my attendance at your Centennial Anniversary. I have no doubt the occasion will be both pleasant and profitable. The Town of Riverhead is the connecting link between the eastern and western towns of our County, and that she will continue to join them together in the future, as in the past, is the hearty wish of the loyal sons of Suffolk.

Yours truly,
W. M. SMITH.

NEW YORK STATE LIBRARY,
ALBANY, June 29, 1892.
MR. JOHN BAGSHAW,
Secretary of the General Committee, etc.:

DEAR SIR:—Your kind invitation to me to be present at celebration of the Centennial of the formation of the Town of Riverhead, on the 4th of July next, was received this morning. I regret to say I had made arrangements to be elsewhere engaged, and, therefore, can only send regrets that I cannot be with you on so interesting occasion. I trust you will do as all the other towns have done, send the State Library a published copy of the proceedings.

Respectfully yours,
GEORGE ROGERS HOWELL.

SOUTHAMPTON, June 29, 1892.
MR. JOHN BAGSHAW, Secretary:

DEAR SIR:—Please accept my thanks for your invitation to be present at the Centennial Anniversary of the formation of your town on the 4th.

It is hardly probable that I can come, but I will do so if possible.

Trusting you will have a good time,
I am, yours truly,
JAMES H. PIERSON.

SOUTHOLD, June 29, 1892.
JOHN BAGSHAW, Esq.:

DEAR SIR:—Most gratefully appreciated is your kind invitation to be present at the Centennial Anniversary of the

7

formation of the Town of Riverhead, on the 4th of July next. It is my purpose to attend the public meeting which you will hold at 2 P. M.

Thankfully yours,

EPHER WHITAKER.

KINGS PARK, June 30, 1892.

JOHN BAGSHAW, Esq., Riverhead, N. Y.:

DEAR SIR:—Your kind invitation at hand. Am sorry to say I cannot come on account of a prior engagement.

However, you have my best wishes that you may have a rousing good time.

Thanking you, I am yours

Very truly,

B. F. CURTIS.

BABYLON, L. I., June 30, 1892.

JOHN BAGSHAW, Esq.:

Your very cordial invitation to attend the Centennial Anniversary of the Town of Riverhead is duly received.

I regret that a previous engagement will prevent my acceptance, for I have no doubt that those present will have a royal good time, and the celebration will be worthy the good old Town of Riverhead.

Yours truly,

RICHARD HIGBIE.

BRIDGE HAMPTON, 30th June, 1892.

JOHN BAGSHAW, Esq.:

DEAR SIR:—Your invitation that I attend the coming Centennial Celebration of the formation of the Town of Riverhead is received, and I am obliged therefor.

It would give me great pleasure to attend the celebration and I intend to do so if my health permits, but that is uncertain.

I am yours truly,

H. P. HEDGES.

SPRINGS, L. I., July 1, 1892.

JOHN BAGSHAW, Esq.:

DEAR SIR:—Accept thanks for the invitation duly received to attend Riverhead's first Centennial Celebration. I regret exceedingly that I cannot be present with you. I extend congratulations, however, that this "Chip of the (South) old

8

block," which had been fashioned into the centre pin of old Suffolk machinery, can call attention to its career with so much honest pride.

Very truly yours,
GEO. A. MILLER.

MR. JOHN BAGSHAW:

DEAR SIR:—Please accept for your committee my thanks for your cordial invitation to be present at the Centennial Anniversary of the formation of your town. I regret that circumstances, over which I have no control, render it impossible for me to be present with you on that day.

Hoping that you may be favored with a perfect day and that your celebration may prove a most gratifying success,

I remain yours,
BYRON GRIFFING.

SHELTER ISLAND HEIGHTS, July 1, 1892.

PATCHOGUE, N. Y., July 1, 1892.

JOHN BAGSHAW, Esq.:

DEAR SIR:—Many thanks for your kind invitation to be present at the Centennial Anniversary of the formation of your Town of Riverhead, on July 4th.

It would afford me pleasure to be present, but visiting friends, who will be in Patchogue over the 4th, will claim my attention, so that I hardly feel justified in being absent on that day.

Yours very truly,
JOHN M. PRICE.

MIDDLE ISLAND, N. Y., July 2, 1892.

MR. JOHN BAGSHAW, Secretary:

DEAR SIR:—Your invitation to attend the Centennial Celebration of the organization of Riverhead Town is received with grateful appreciation of the honor thereby conferred upon me. I have always felt a deep interest in Riverhead as a model town in many of its points of character, and should take great pleasure in attending the celebration. Circumstances may favor my doing so.

I am, yours respectfully,
RICHARD M. BAYLES.

After another selection from the choir, Miss Minerva Mitchell read the immortal Declaration of Independence. The

9

historical paper which followed, after music by the band, pre-
pared and read by Orville B. Ackerly, Esq., now a resident of
Yonkers, N. Y., is here given in full:

Mr. Chairman, Ladies and Gentlemen:

We have been passing through a period of centennial anniversaries, the first in our history as a nation. Beginning
with the celebration of the Declaration of our Independance
at Philadelphia in 1876, which must always remain the greatest
event in our national life, our birth; hardly a week, certainly
not a month, has passed, that has not witnessed in some part
of the territory comprising the original thirteen States the
centennial anniversary of some important event: the battles
on land or sea, victories or defeats of the Revolutionary War,
the final surrender of Cornwallis, the evacuation of New York,
the adoption of the Constitution, the inauguration of President
Washington, and like events, so that, as much as possible, we
have lived over again the stormy scenes of our early history,
and we appreciate more than ever before what it cost to make
us a free and independent nation. In many places, celebration
of events that took place two hundred years ago have occurred.
The county celebrated its bi-centennial nine years ago, and
the towns of Southold and Southampton only two years ago
rejoiced over the fact that they had lived two hundred and
fifty years. Last autumn the churches at Upper Aquebogue
and Baiting Hollow invited their friends to enjoy with them in
the festivities that appropriately marked the conclusion of one
hundred years of useful existence, and now the Town of Riverhead finding itself one hundred years old, proposes to celebrate the fact, selecting the glorious national anniversary day,
that the fires of local pride and national patriotism may mingle
and make brighter and more memorable the happy occasion.
Next year this notable period of anniversaries may be said
to close with the celebration of the greatest event known to
modern times, that which made all the rest possible—the
discovery of a new world by Columbus. Occurring somewhat

tardily, it may be all the more successful. No lover of his kind and of his country but rejoices over the fact that the public enters so heartily into the spirit of these celebrations.

Let us consider briefly the condition of our own country and the world at large at the time this town was organized. The new constitution was almost an experiment, for less than four years had passed since it had been made the supreme law of the land. No addition had been made to our territory. Maine was still a province of Massachusetts, and Vermont had just been made a State only to prevent it from any longer being debatable ground between New York and New Hampshire. The vast valley of the Mississippi was a part of France, while Florida and the immense region north of the Rio Grande were still under the rule of Spain. Thanks to enterprising and intrepid explorers, we to-day know a great deal about Central Africa. But the generation that lived when this town was established knew nothing of the unknown land beyond the Mississippi. In all maps of the world at that time the region was a blank. It was, of course, supposed that there must be rivers and mountains there, and so they were put down apparently at random and by guess-work. It was the custom of geographers to people these unknown wastes with strange and uncouth animals, or monsters rather, which makes one of the poets of that day declare,

> " Geographers on Afric maps
> With savage pictures fill their gaps;
> O'er uninhabitable downs
> Place elephants for want of towns."

And it was so on the maps of America. The "western country" meant then the middle of the State of New York. New York was a respectable sized city of about 30,000 inhabitants, where everybody knew everybody, and on the east end of Long Island there were many who had heard of the great city and longed to see it, but "died without the sight," for want of courage enough to brave the long and dangerous journey. George Washington was serving his first term as President, and "His Excellency, George Clinton, Esq.," was our Governor. The great men of state were Alexander Hamilton, Aaron Burr, Robert R. Livingston, John Jay and Gouverneur Morris; De Witt Clinton was but a young lawyer only five years out of college. Fulton had not yet made the dream of his life a reality; the sloop on the river and the stage coach on the land were the means of conveyance, and the only means. Political parties had no platforms, at least no written ones, but the dividing line between the Federalists and Republicans were as strongly drawn as any party lines at the present time. The followers of Jefferson and Burr denounced Washington and Hamilton in terms which would be considered outrageous even to the political rancour of to-day, while they in return were accused in most vehement language of a base conspiracy to destroy religion, the Bible and all that respectability then held dear, and to emulate the Jacobins of France in their deeds of blood. George III. was still the King of Great Britain, and destined to continue so for a score of years to come. Louis XVI. and his ill-fated Queen, Marie Antoinette, were still the rulers of France, but only in name, for the time was brief indeed before they would leave the palace for the prison, and the prison for the scaffold. Robespierre was but a young attorney, and had not yet made his name infamous for all coming time. Mirabeau, whose power and political genius might have turned the tide of revolution into more peaceful channels, had but lately passed away. The French philosophers, who had done their best (or their worse) to destroy all faith in religion and the Bible, and had conjured up in their place atheism and anarchy, were destined soon to be among the first victims of the fiends they had raised. Among the spectators of the events that "passed with giant steps" was a young man maned Napoleon Bonaparte, then twenty-three years old, a captain of artillery, who was shortly to change the map of Europe and make the earth shake with the tread of his armies. Wellesley, afterwards the Iron Duke, Napoleon's conqueror to be, was twenty-two years of age and preparing for service in India. Spain was then but a shadow of the power that had been, but even then how vast was its territory. Prussia had become powerful through the mighty military genius of Frederick the Great, but what is now the German Empire was then but a group of petty States powerless for want of union. Italy, partly ruled as "the States of the Church," partly under independent rulers, and all over-shadowed by Austria. The only place in Europe where freedom was enshrined was on the mountain top of Switzer-land. Turkey was not then the "sick man of Europe," but a power fully capable of taking care of itself. Greece was but a name on the map; it had its ruins and its records of the past, nothing else. It now seems hardly credible that the piratical fleets of Algiers, Tunis and Tripoli were then the terror of the seas, and the most powerful nations of Christen-dom were compelled to pay them tribute as a protection for their commerce. It was the beginning of a new order of things when the young nation beyond the Atlantic returned as an answer to their demands, "Millions for defense, but not one cent for tribute." Lastly there was Russia, vast in its extent of land, great in the numbers of its people, but as a nation just emerging from barbarism, and with a young Alex-ander for an Emperor. We might add as an item of interest, that when this town was established, the first newspaper on Long Island was but a year old, *Frothingham's Long Island Herald*, established at Sag Harbor, May 10, 1791.

Seventeen hundred and ninety-two seems to have been a year prolific of events worth noting. Kentucky, created a State out of Virginia's large territory, was that year admitted to the Union, becoming the fifteenth State. The manufacturing city of Paterson, N. J., was founded that year and is now celebrating the fact. A Boston captain, cruising in the Pacific, by acci-dent discovered the largest river on the coast, and named it after his ship, the Columbia. The New York Stock Exchange was started that year; coal gas was first used as an illuminant, and the canal system of this State originated in 1792. And down at East Hampton, in a very humble dwelling, on the 9th day of June, in that year, to the first teacher of Clinton Academy, the first academy in this State, there was born a son, who, in a wandering, checkered career covering sixty years, as clerk, actor, manager, playwriter and diplomat, achieved nothing else of note, but made himself famous as long as the English tongue shall last, as the author of "Home, Sweet Home"—John Howard Payne.

On January 11, 1792, there was presented to the Assembly, then in session in New York City, the petition of Peter Reeves and others that the town of Southold be divided into two towns. At the same time, the petition of John Wells, Justice of the Peace, and others praying for a postponement of such action by the Legislature, until the next session, was read. Benjamin Horton, Jr., Henry Herrick and others also prayed for an Act authorizing town meetings to be held alternately at the old Town Meeting House (the First Presbyterian Church at Southold) and the Aquebogue Meeting House. The last refers doubtless to the old church, 24x33, which then stood on the south side of the road, nearly opposite the present church at Upper Aquebogue. The petitions were referred to the appropriate committee, which reported on the 16th of the following month in favor of an Act dividing the town, and the Assembly concurred. The Act passed the House March 3, and passed the Senate five days later. The law was approved by the Council of Revision, a feature in our first constitution, and Riverhead became a town March 13, 1792. These petitions cannot be found, and we are left to surmise the reasons for and against the change. No matter what they were, the town became a fact, and she has no doubt as to the date of her birth, unlike her mother, Southold, and her aunt, Southampton; for these dear old sisters, having long passed the period when ladies expect to be thought young, are now claiming, each that she is older than the other. On this question Riverhead is neutral; in fact, we do not want it settled; it keeps alive interest and stimulates inquiry, benefiting us by increasing our knowledge of the beginnings of history on the east end of Long Island.

The first town meeting was held at the Court House (the old Court House) April 3, 1792, and Daniel Wells was chosen Supervisor; Josiah Reeve, Town Clerk; John C. Terry, Joseph Wells and Benjamin Terry, Assessors; Jeremiah Wells and Spencer Dayton, Highway Commissioners; Deacon Daniel Terry, Zachariah Hallock and Daniel Edwards, Overseers of the Poor; Nathan Youngs, Eleazer Luce, Rufus Youngs, John Corwin, Zophar Mills, Peter Reeve and Merrit Howell, Overseers of Highways; Sylvanus Brown, Collector, and David Brown, Abel Corwin and Benjamin Horton, Constables. These names sound familiar; for although all long since dead, others bearing the same names, certainly same surnames, are among us to-day. In later years new and strange names have appeared on the town tickets, like Perkins, Millard, Stackpole, Homan and Bagshaw, but only because the people are hospitable, unselfish and like to encourage immigration. Daniel Wells, the first Supervisor, was re-elected the next year, but died before completing the term of office. Josiah Reeve continued to be Town Clerk for four years, and was succeeded by John Woodhull (afterwards Judge John Woodhull), who held the office for eleven years.

In the early days the circumstances and conditions of establishing a new village or settlement were very different from those of the present time. The main points to be considered then were: How near to a bay or harbor? Is there plenty of meadow land? This was a most important consideration, for the crop of meadow hay which, without care or cultivation, came with annual regularity, was a thing of the greatest value. And last, not by any means least, "Is there a stream for a mill?" How greatly times have changed may be known by the fact that when a country place is now spoken of as a desirable place of residence the very first interrogatory is, "How far from a railroad station?"

The main settlement of Setauket, the parent hive of the

15

town of Brookhaven, soon sent out small swarms of inhabitants to establish new villages. The native Indian inhabitants have a right to the soil, which, to their credit be it said, the settlers of the towns in Suffolk County never failed to recognize, and under date of June 10, 1694, we find that the Indian Sachem, "John Mayhew, doth freely give, grant and surrender, unto the Committee of Connecticut for settling business on Long Island, for the use of the town of Seatalk, the feed and timber of all ye lands from ye Old Man's to the Wading River." This was signed by the Sachem and duly witnessed by John Cooper and Richard Howell, who were prominent residents of the village of Southampton. This John Mayhew, an Indian with an English name, must have been a powerful chief and well recognized as one in authority, for we find him giving to the original purchasers of Moriches their right and title to the land, and his name is connected with other transfers on the south side of the land.

In 1669 and 1686 the settlers of Setauket obtained from the Royal Governor patents for "all the lands, bays, harbors and streams between the Stony Brook River on the west and the head of Wading River or Red Creek on the east," " and from the head of the Wading River their eastern bounds were to be a straight line running due north to the sound and due south to the sea or main ocean." Our first knowledge, then, of the Wading River and the settlement near it, finds it as a part of the town of Brookhaven. The spot which was then designated as " the head of the Wading River," was marked by a large pepperidge tree which after standing for more than a century and a half fell to decay, and the site it occupied was in 1840 marked by a stone bearing the initial letters of the adjoining towns. It stands at the northwest corner of the church lot and will doubtless remain for long years to come. The land at the Wading River having been fairly bought, next comes the settlement, and as the record states, " At a lawful town meeting 17 November, 1671, it was voted and agreed upon that there shall be a village at the Wading

River or thereabouts of eight families or eight men. It was granted and agreed upon by a vote that Daniel Lane, Jr., shall have a lotment at the Wading River convenient to the water for his calling (they do not tell us what that calling was), and at the same time allotments were granted to Thomas Jenness, Elias Bayles, Joseph Longbottom and Thomas Smith, and Francis Muncy had a lot granted there with the rest upon condition that he lived there himself!" Was this a shrewd dodge to get Francis Muncy (who may have been an undesirable neighbor) as far off from Setauket as they could, or was it an equally shrewd dodge on his part to get a lot free without ever having to live on it? These are questions upon which history throws no light and we cannot assume to answer them. From that time the village was an established fact. The Wading River is cetainly the smallest stream ever dignified with that title, for its entire length from mouth to fountain head cannot much exceed a mile, but the place has always been one of the most important portions of our town, though comparatively far greater in the past than in the present; but that it will have a prosperous future no one who sees its natural beauties can doubt.

In 1675 there is another Indian grant to the patentees of Brookhaven, ratifying and confirming all former purchases of land between Stony Brook and the Wading River, and by the same grant all lands not before purchased were conveyed to Richard Woodhull. This grant was signed by the Sachem, John Mayhew, and his associates Masstuse, Nascenge and Achedouse. On November 23, 1675, Richard Woodhull relinquishes all the said lands to the towns and under the same date we find the following: "At a town meeting was voted and given to Richard Woodhull a farm at the Wading River, that is to say, ten acres upland where it is most convenient to set a house on, and three score and ten acres more of upland where the said Richard Woodhull shall choose it, lying together adjacent to the said Wading River, and half the meadow that belongs to us this side of the creek, being divided, and to draw cuts for it, and this is given in consideration of land that was given by the Indians and assigned over to the towns."

To locate ancient landmarks is one of the duties, and we need not say one of the greatest pleasures, of the antiquarian, and our researches lead us to believe that the place mentioned as the " ten acres where it is most convenient to set a house up " is the present homestead of Charles Woodhull, the descendant in the eighth generation from Brookhaven's most illustrious founder.

On May 4, 1708, we find that upon application of John Roe, Jr., in behalf of himself and others of the Wading River, that "they may have liberty to set up a grist mill at the Red Brook there, and to take up —— acres of land adjoining to it for the use of the said mill or miller, on condition they set up a mill as aforesaid and support the same continually." The Red Brook, so called from the color of the sands over which it flows, still "goes on forever," and the mill, under a long succession of various owners, still grinds as it did in days of yore. How Wading River came to be a part of Southold is a curious episode in our local history. It seems that about 1708, one John Rogers, who had been a townsman of Brookhaven, had removed to the town of Southold and by various misfortunes had become a public charge. Southold claimed, and with justice, that the cost of his support was chargeable to the neighboring town whence he came. A letter was sent by the authorities of Southold calling attention to the matter, and on October 7, 1708, a reply was ordered to be sent. This elicited another letter from Southold, and on December 9, another reply was sent. The evidence was plainly against Brookhaven, for, at a Trustee meeting in June, 1709, we find the following resolution :

" Upon the application of James Reeve, in behalf of the town of Southold in reference to defray the charge of keeping John Rogers, it was agreed upon between the said James Reeve on the one part in the part of Southold and the Trustees of Brookhaven on the other part, that the town of Brookhaven shall be acquitted and fully discharged from all charges whatever that now is or shall hereafter be concerning the said John Rogers, his keeping or care, on the condition that the town of Brookhaven do assign unto the town of Southold all their patent right of the land and meadow on the east side of the Wading River, and also pay unto the said James Reeve, four pounds in current money at his house, for the use of the town of Southold, at or before the 29th day of September next ensuing the date hereof."

Now we think our readers will, one and all, agree that Southold, through James Reeve, its agent, made a pretty profitable bargain, and this is the first instance on record where a pauper added to the wealth of a town. And so it happened that the due north line from the pepperidge tree to the sound ceased to be a boundary and the river itself became our western bounds.

Our limits will not permit us to dwell too long on the ancient history of this village; let it suffice to mention some of the names of men who were prominent, and of places that were well known localities at the time when our town was established. We might say that from the earliest settlement the Woodhull family were the bone and sinew of the village. Here was the homestead of Joshua Woodhull, who died in 1787 at the age of fifty-two years. He was well known here during the days of the Revolution, and on the top of his house was built a lookout from which the watcher could descry and give timely warning if marauding bands from British vessels on the sound were seen approaching the shore. Not far from him, on the present homestead of Mrs. Thomas Coles, and what was in the very early days the home of Robert Terry, lived his son, Nathaniel Woodhull, a true and worthy representative of a noble race, a strong supporter of the church, a good, substantial citizen, and in all the relations of life a useful and honored man. He was the maternal grandfather of our worthy chairman, Nathaniel Woodhull Foster, and from whom he derives his honored name. On the east side of the street, in the centre of the village, was the homestead and extensive farm of Major Frederick Hudson, a wealthy and influential citizen, but of Tory proclivities, and the officers of the British army found a warm welcome at his house. His son, Oliver Hudson, sold the estate to Zophar Mills, who was one

19

of the largest land owners in the town. To all lovers of local history there is a peculiar interest connected with this farm, from the fact that it was the early home of the famous Indian preacher, Paul Cuffee, who was the bound servant of Major Hudson till his twenty-first year. Strange change of circumstances. The grave of the master is somewhere unmarked and unknown in a dense thicket of weeds and briars. The grave of the servant, fenced and guarded with pious care, by the roadside at Good Ground, is visited by hundreds who revere his virtues and honor his name. Further east is the well-known homestead of Zophar Miller, whose son, Sylvester, and grandson, Elihu, are names "whom not to know argues a Riverheader unknown." In front of this house, and a few feet north of the road, stood the old meeting house built about 1785. It stood till 1838, when it was sold and removed, and is now a barn on the premises of Alonzo Hulse, about two and a half miles east of the village. When the new church was built in 1857 it was Zophar Miller who gave the lot for the new edifice. It was in the house of the Miller family that the post-office was kept for sixty-one years. It was removed in 1886 to its present location. One of the conspicuous features of the place is the ancient house of Stephen Homan (of an old East-Hampton family), who came here in the latter part of the last century, married a daughter of Zophar Mills, and was store-keeper, tavern-keeper and farmer. A brown tombstone tells us he died in 1816 at the age of forty-nine. His son, Benjamin Homan, who never tires of talking of the past, inherits his name and place. There, too, in old times, was Isaac Reeve, a noted boatman and great judge and prognosticator of wind and weather. For aught we know he may have been a descendant of James Reeve who drove so sharp a bargain for the town. And also Nathaniel Tuthill, a well known citizen, and as one of the old residents said, "a mighty smart man," and father of our honored townsman, Hon. James H. Tuthill. What shall we say of Jonathan Worth, who for long years ran the mill, and then left it to his son David, who sold it to a company consisting of the minister, Partial Terry, Deacon Nathaniel Tuthill, Deacon Nathaniel Woodhull and Deacon Luther Brown. Church and State might be separate, but church and mill were pretty closely connected in those days. The sentiment of the people may be imagined when we learn that when Washington was a candidate for re-election to the Presidency he had only three votes in Wading River, and these were cast by Rev. David Wells, Stephen Homan and Benjamin Worth. New York took no part in the election of the first President.

The changes which are apparent in every part of Long Island, are especially evident in the relative importance of villages in the present compared with the past. At the time when this town was established let us suppose a stranger had asked, " What is your most important place? " The answer might have been, " Wading River or Aquebogue," but it most assuredly would not have been " Riverhead." In the olden time to live on the post road had a certain advantage. There would always be more or less passing. The stage coach with its weekly or semi-weekly mail was the only communication with the outside world, and its arrival would be looked for with an interest which we can now scarcely realize. The taverns at intervals of a few miles with their swinging signs announcing "Accommodations for Man and Beast," were welcome sights to the belated traveler. But the greater part of the people did not travel; many of them scarcely ever went beyond the bounds of their native village, and it is safe to say that hundreds lived, and lived to a good old age, who never saw anything outside of Suffolk County. The foundation for a village was a fertile soil where good crops could be raised. Means of communication with other villages were of little importance. As one old man expressed it, "A place is made to stay in, not go away from." It was the boast of some old-fashioned farmers that they did not go off their farm any day of the week except Sunday. The railroad changed all this. The whole section of country in the neighborhood of Riverhead was known to the old settlers by the name of Occobog, a name common to both sides of the river, and meaning in the Indian language, "the place at the head of the bay, or the cove place." Previous to 1659, John Tucker, a very prominent man in the early days, and who was dignified with the title of Deacon, Captain and Esquire at a time when they meant something, presented a petition for the the privilege of building a saw-mill within the town bounds near the head of the river. It was granted with liberty to "cut all sorts of timber," but with the condition that he should "cut no more oak than fell in the common track of getting pine and cedar, which was the chief inducement of getting a mill there to saw." This would seem to indicate that oak was comparatively scarce. He also asked for " ten acres of land for himself and such partners as he should take in to himself," which was granted. He seems to have found a partner in the person of Joseph Horton, for on February 7, 1659, we find that " John Tucker with Joseph Horton desire the five men to enlarge the grant to the effect that they should have the privilege of building the saw-mill and of cutting timber for twenty-one years without molestation, nor any inhabitant to set up another mill by them.". This also was granted on condition of their completing the mill within three years.

A writer in the Genealogical and Biographical Record (Oct., 1882) claims that Joseph Carpenter of Maschete Cove, Long Island, who built a saw and fulling mill in 1677, " was the first man on Long Island, New York, Connecticut or New Jersey, to set up a saw-mill run by water power," but here was a mill running more than fifteen years before, and the credit of being the first to establish a mill of this kind must now be given to John Tucker and Joseph Horton and to Riverhead. Tucker lived here in 1665 and was no doubt the first settler, but we cannot be certain of the exact location of his house. The town of Southampton, on April 14, 1693, granted to John Wick, " serge dresser," " the use of the stream called the Little River, on condition of setting up a fulling mill, and fulling cloth for that town and Southold." It is doubtful if he complied with the conditions, for two years later we find that Southampton voted that John Parker and his heirs and assigns should have the stream and the privileges granted to John Wick, on condition of his building a good fulling mill, and that he should full cloth there "forever." John Parker also had land granted to him in 1700 to build a house on, and he probably did build a temporary residence at that time, but in 1713 he built a far more substantial mansion, which is yet standing on the south side of the river, and which in after years passed into the hands of his son-in-law, Wm. Albertson, and continued in his family for three or four generations. Since then this house was owned and occupied by the Sweezy family and is now the residence of Sylvester H. Woodhull. On May 15, 1715, we find that "the Justices of Suffolk County met at Parker's to ascertain the amount of arrears of taxes."

All the lands of Peconic River which are included in the village are a part of the original division of the lands of South-old, called the second Division of Aquebank lands. The lots were of large extent and ran from the river to the sound. In 1711 John Parker purchased from John Tucker, a grandson of the original John Tucker who died in 1690, one of the original lots containing 400 acres, bounded west by land of Widow Margaret Cooper and east by land of John Parker, which seems to have been another original lot of the same size, and which he had bought from its former owner. These two lots, with a lot of Widow Cooper on the west, embrace the entire business portion of Riverhead.

In January, 1727, about a month before his death, John Parker gave a deed of gift to his daughter Abigail and her husband, Joseph Wickham, Jr., for their lives and then to her heirs, for all his land north of the river, and this tract in course of time came into possession of Parker Wickham, their eldest son and heir-at-law, whose loyalist proclivities caused his estate to be confiscated after the Revolution and sold to Nathaniel Norton, who sold a part of it to Stephen Jagger, and it is well known in recent years as the " Jagger farm." There are missing links in the chain of title which more extended investigation may supply; but it seems as if at some time previous to 1727 a tract of 130 acres on the western part of this land had been disposed of to other parties, for in 1753 Thomas Fanning sold John Griffing " a tract of land at a place called Acaboug, bounded north and east by the lands of Abigail Wickham, south by and with Peconick river, together with the dwelling thereon, so far as the saw-mill, and west by the land of Christopher Young, containing by estimates 130 acres, reserving one-half acre of land at and about the place where his mother lies buried, with free passage in and to the same." This burial place, doubtless the first in the village, is situated just north of and adjoining the stable on the lot of Mrs. Louisa Howell on the east side of Griffing Avenue and next south of the railroad. The dwelling house mentioned is the first of which we have any positive knowledge in the village, and the Long Island House now occupies its site. The deed evidently includes the stream.

This John Griffing, the first of his name to settle in Riverhead, was a prominent Whig. At the request of his neighbors he became a "tea-spy," as they called men whose business it was to detect and prevent the use of tea and other imported articles upon which the English Government levied duties of the inhabitants here. When the British forces got possession of Long Island after their victory over the Colonist forces at Brooklyn in August, 1766, Mr. Griffing and many others fled to Connecticut. He died there October 18, 1777, in the sixty-first year of his age. As he died without will his property descended to his son and namesake. The mother of the late Charles and Gamaliel Vail was one of his daughters, and we well remember hearing them comment on the injustice of the English law of primogeniture. His grave is at a place called Cromwell, on the west side of the Connecticut River, about three miles above Middletown. Near it is the grave of Martha L'Hommedieu, the mother of Ezra L'Hommedieu, one of the most prominent men in the State 100 years ago, and a resident of Southold until his death in 1811. The land next west of the Griffing farm, the original lot of Widow Margaret Cooper, descended to her grandchildren, the children of Stephen Bailey and Elnathan Topping of Southampton. Upon a division of her estate the land above mentioned fell to the latter, beyond which we cannot trace it, but in 1753 it was owned wholly or in part by Christopher Young. For long years the place was isolated from the rest of the town. No direct road connected it with the "Middle Road," then the principal thoroughfare. The fulling mill, the grist mill and the Court House and jail were the only things to call any of the people from the neighboring regions, and the people whose business called them there did not come to stay. It was recognized as a very central locality in the county, and this is doubtless the reason why the place was selected for the county seat. On November 25, 1727, an Act was passed by the Governor and Provincial Legislature to enable the Justices of the Peace in the County of Suffolk to build a "County House and Prison." Riverhead was chosen as the most suitable place, and the building was erected and the first court held in it on March 27, 1729. Previous to that the jail seems to have been the basement or cellar of the old church at Southold.

On July 12, 1729, an Act was passed reciting that "there had been of late some dispute among the Supervisors of the County of Suffolk," and hence it was enacted "that the place and time of the Supervisors' meeting forever hereafter should be at the Court House on the last Tuesday in the month of October, and that their pay should be 9 shillings (or $1.12 1-2) a day." For a period of more than seventy-five years the place remained stationary, and from the best authorities we learn that for nearly thirty years after the Revolution there were but four houses, the Griffing tavern, Joseph Wickham's house, afterwards that of David Jagger. David Horton lived in the Court House and kept the jail. Stephen Griffing occupied the place late of Dr. Thomas Osborn, and besides these there was the old Parker house, then owned by William Albertson on the other side of the river. It may perhaps be needless to state that till within comparatively recent times the village was surrounded by a dense forest. One of our best known citizens, John P. Terry, says: "When a boy (sixty years ago), I set snares and caught quails where the house of Hon. James H. Tuthill now stands. All the land north of Main Street was covered with woods, except in a few spots." He adds as a curious illustration of the changes in social life: "Sixty-one years ago my father died, one of the well-known men of the place. His funeral expenses were a dollar and a half. The remains, and the mourners, the members of his family, all rode to the grave in the same box wagon. The grave was dug by neighbors who volunteered; and this was the general custom at the time." He adds: "I saw ten deer, which had been caught in the woods south of the river, confined in a pen where Riverhead Hall now stands. The first store was in the northeast corner of the house of the late Judge Miller. It was kept by Stephen Griffing, who afterwards moved to West Hampton. Seventy years ago, Jasper or 'Jep' Vail lived at Riverhead, but kept a store some miles east, opposite the Steeple Church, thinking that a far better location for business than this place. He had some peculiar methods: for instance, if a customer tendered a dollar bill for fifty cents worth of goods he would cut the bill in two, keep one-half and tell the customer to bring the other half some other time, and he would take it for fifty cents. He thus secured that man's custom for so much trade anyhow, and then he would paste the two halves together. The use of liquor was general. All storekeepers kept it and everybody drank it, and to expect a workingman to live without rum was the same as expecting him to live without air." For nearly a century and a half the Griffing family had been part and parcel of the place, and none have been more closely connected with its business and social interests. One of our largest hotels, kept by a member of the family, stands on the land bought by his ancestor in 1753, and one of the finest streets is justly named in their honor. Dr. Thomas Osborn was the first physician in the village and is well remembered by the older citizens. He commenced practice very early in the present century, and died here in 1849. Sixty years ago there was but one mail a week, brought here in a one-horse wagon. If a person wished to go to New York he must cross over to Quogue, take the mail stage which came from Sag Harbor, and he would reach the city at the close of the second day. A newspaper clipping tells us that "on the 25th day of July, 1844, the first train passed over the Long Island Railroad from Brooklyn to Greenport, and the event was duly celebrated." Well it might be. It was the commencement of a new order of things. Since then Riverhead has been a part of the world.

At the Upper Mills there had been at various times a grist mill, a saw-mill, and a fulling mill, all owned by Richard Albertson, and his son after him, and built in the latter part of the last century. In 1828 John Perkins became the proprietor of the water-power and established a business there that has been for long years one of the most important industries. With that honesty and enterprise that have ever distinguished them, the name became a household word in all parts of Suffolk County. "If you buy Perkins' cloth," said an old farmer, "you know what you have got, but if you buy this store cloth it will like enough drop off of you in the street." No such catastrophe ever occurred with cloth that was made at the Upper Mills.

Sixty years ago there were about thirty houses in all scattered along the main road, and outside of the main street there was not a dwelling of any description. Cutting wood and shipping it on small vessels was the most important industry and employed more men during the winter than any other enterprise. As the level of the street was much lower then, it was no uncommon thing for the tide to come up to the old Court

House: and there are now living in this village two ladies who, when young, picked huckleberries in a swamp where Bridge Street now is—Mrs. Daniel R. Edwards and Mrs. Noah W. Hallock. Some seventy years ago the house of the late David Jagger was moved from the " Middle Road." To accomplish this it was necessary to move it east to the fork of the roads and then west to Riverhead. It was quite an event and required a great many yoke of oxen.

It can be readily understood that the population here was far too small to constitute a church or to justify the erection of a meeting-house. As late as 1828 the people from Flanders, Riverhead, Baiting Hollow, Northville and east as far as Mattituck, went to the Steeple Church at Upper Aquebogue to worship. But a volume could be written to tell the lives and labors of a class of reverent preachers who, with small reward for constant labor, made it the object of their lives to do good. Their meetings were held in barns, schoolhouses, private residences, and even in the open air, and their coming was anxiously awaited. The Steeple Church might be called the mother of churches. It was a portion of this congregation that in 1829 built a small meeting-house about two miles east of this village. In 1834 this congregation was also divided, one portion taking the meeting-house, removing it to Northville. The remainder established a church in Riverhead, and at first worshipped in the lower room of the Seminary building, till the erection of the Congregational Church in 1841. But prior to this came the Methodist Church, with its untiring ministry. This society was organized in 1833, and the first meeting-house built in 1834, to be succeeded in 1870 by the the present elegant edifice. The followers of Emanuel Swedenborg organized a society in 1839 and built a house of worship in 1855. The old Court House, or County Hall, as it was generally called, might, in the early days, have well been called a church of all denominations. The Congregational Church of Upper Aquebogue always claimed this neighborhood as a part of their parish, and every other Sunday Mr.

Sweezy, the pastor, would preach in the building. Next came the Methodist circuit rider, who would preach on Friday afternoon or evening, making his temporary home (for he had no abiding one) at the house of Dr. Osborn; and at a later day, the service of the Roman Catholic Church would be conducted in the same place, their church being built in 1870. The Free Methodists built their church in 1872. The Episcopalians commenced stated worship in 1870, and erected a chapel in 1873. So far all these varied denominations have lived in harmony, which we trust will never be interrupted.

For long years the schools were of the most inferior description; the only ones that had the slightest claim to being educational institutions being schools kept at Upper and Lower Aquebogue, the former by Josiah Reeve, who was afterward Sheriff of the county, and the latter by Judge David Warner. These had a well-deserved reputation, and their influence for good was felt far and wide.

Riverhead, and indeed Suffolk County, is indebted to the late Judge George Miller for much that is good, but in nothing is it under greater obligation that for the seminary established by him in 1834 to advance the cause of female education. It was from the commencement a complete success, and its influence for good can be hardly expressed in words. It is fortunate for the present generation that the days of the old-fashioned district school have passed away, and it is to be hoped that the entire community fully appreciates the advantages of the Union School and the tireless labors of our well-trained and efficient teachers.

We must not fail to give our due meed of praise to the followers of the "art preservative of arts." Our first newspaper, the *Suffolk Gazette*, was started in August, 1849, under the editorial management of John Hancock. The next year it was removed to Sag Harbor, but came back to its native place in 1854, and ended its career shortly after. Then came the *Suffolk Union*, with Washington Van Zandt as editor, in 1859, a very fearless paper during the early days of the Civil

War. The office, which stood on the south side of Main Street, just west of the residence of the late Dr. Luce, was burned about thirty years ago and publication stopped. A few years afterward, Buel G. Davis, an energetic young man from Greenport, started the *Monitor* here, but it did not continue long, being purchased by James S. Evans, who merged it in a paper he was publishing in Setauket, which establishment was afterwards removed to Patchogue and survives to-day in the *Patchogue Advance*. Then James B. Slade, started in a very modest way what he called an advertising sheet, which grew into the *Riverhead News*. In 1875, Wm. R. Duvall purchased the *News* and continued it till the time of his death in 1882. Mr. Duvall was a witty, sarcastic and effective writer, and humorous as well, though, strange to say, he seldom smiled. He had traveled a great deal and had a wide knowledge of the world and men. His son and namesake succeeded to his work and well maintains the character and influence of the paper.

We cannot do better than to present a picture of Riverhead as it was fifty years ago, as taken from notes kindly furnished by Hon. Henry P. Hedges, who has been so long identified with the public life of Suffolk County, and who came here fresh from college to study law with Judge Miller. He says:

"I went to Riverhead in October, 1840, when the Harrison campaign 'log cabin and hard cider' cries were heard. At that time Henry T. Penney and John Corwin kept the hotels. Penney was Deputy Sheriff and kept a hotel in an old-fashioned house formerly of his father-in-law, William Griffing, the father of Wells and Hubbard Griffing. At that time there were about forty houses in Riverhead. Dr. Osborn's was almost the extreme west, only one or two houses beyond it. The avenue to the railroad station was then a cart path, and where the Court House now stands was thick woods. My solitary walk was often over that cart path, north to where is now the cemetery. At that time the

Griffings were shipping wood to Providence; Judge Miller was in the thick of his professional fight; Sidney L. Griffin was the only other lawyer in Riverhead; Dr. Thomas Osborn was in active practice as a physician and so was Dr. Doane; Capt. Edward Vail was running a vessel, also Capt. Harry Horton and James Horton; William Jagger and David Jagger were advocating temperance; their father, David, was then living; Herman D. Foster, Elijah Terry and Nathan Corwin were selling goods in country stores; David Davis was building vessels; Timothy Aldrich was building the church; Rev. C. J. Knowles was minister; Clem. Hempstead was painting houses and wagons; Mulford Moore was blacksmithing; Geo. Halsey was tailoring; Titus Conklin was making shoes; and Aunt Polly Griffing was doing then, as always, the work of the good Samaritan; Daniel Edwards, was keeping the jail; John Perkins was manufacturing cloth at the Upper Mills; Isaac Sweezy, across the river, was grinding grain, and John P. Terry, now of the Long Island House, was living with him and threshing rye with a flail.

"The County Courts were held three times a year. Hugh Halsey was first Judge. Henry Landon, Judge Gillett and Richard M. Conkling were among the Associate Judges, and Selah B. Strong was District Attorney. The principal lawyers who came to court were S. S. Gardiner of Shelter Island and Samuel L. Gardiner of Sag Harbor, and Abraham T. Rose. These were the only ones from the east. From the west were Selah B. Strong, Judge Buffett, Charles A. Floyd, and a little later John G. Floyd. The old Court House and jail is now occupied by the Perkins Bros. as a clothing store. Charles Vail and his brother Gamaliel were old residents in the same house, where they continued for many years; now the house of D. F. Vail. North of the Main Street there were no houses, nor on any street parallel with the Main Street. The religious meetings were held in what was called the lecture room, where the Congregational Church now stands. The Ladies' Seminary was taught by Mrs. Miller, and was located

on the same lot. In 1841, the 3d of April, I find a memo-
randum: 'Day before yesterday raised meeting-house in Riverhead.' On December 1, same year, it was dedicated. Mr.
Badger, Secretary of the Home Missionary Society, spoke
from the text, "It is none other than the house of God.'
Hubbard and Wells Griffing were among the most munificent
contributors to that church. There came from Flanders to
trade the peculiar characteristic people from that section—the
old preacher, Nathaniel Fanning, who built his own church,
old Major David Brown and 'Uncle Joe' Goodale. These
two were rivals for the control of Flanders. At that time
David Edwards was Justice, a very competent man and so
mild-mannered that he never offended anyone. In some cases
there would be testimony absolutely conflicting, and plain per-
jury on one and sometimes on both sides. He would allude
to this in his charge as 'a little discrepancy between the evidence for plaintiff and defendant.' He was a great admirer of
the works of Pope, especially the 'Essay on Man.' One of
the men of stronger intellect, and who impressed his opinions very largely upon his companions, was Elijah Terry.
Johnson was the first man that I saw hung in the county. He
did not look like a malicious man. I think Judge Rose de-
fended him. I remember Judge D. G. Gillett of Patchogue,
who came to Riverhead and attended conventions. He was a
large, thick-set man and of very impressive appearance;
and also Dr. Fred. W. Lord, a man of powerful intellect and
pre-eminent as a public speaker. In 1840 Judge Abraham T.
Rose was the most accomplished speaker, politically and as an
advocate before a jury, in this county. It was said that Chan-
cellor Kent once came down to Riverhead to hold a court of
Oyer and Terminer, but found no lawyer, no cases, no prisoner,
and adjourned for want of business. Titus Conklin was very
intelligent, benevolent, and an active man in the church and
business, and he had as fellow workers Deacon Hubbard Griffing, Wells Griffing, Isaac Sweezy, Herman D. Foster and
first of all, Judge George Miller, who for a long time held

32

meetings in the Court House and conducted the services. He was the founder and upholder of the Congregational Church: the Methodist Church was upheld by John Perkins and his family, and Dr. Osborn, who were its main supporters. Jonathan Horton preached in the Swederborgian Church, and was the heart of that organization. Sells Edwards employed him to draw his will. It was intended to give a life estate to a prodigal son, but by a mistake he gave him the whole fee of his portion. Judge Miller used to say Sells Edwards saved 50 cents in writing a will and lost $10,000. Sylvester Miller was a man of excellent understanding. He was Justice of the Peace and Supervisor for many years. He was prudent, with a strong sense of justice, and was fully competent to control and direct. Judge John Woodhull was a man rather intelligent, cautious and discreet, not disposed to yield to the popular current, and more disposed to row against than with it. He was thoroughly honest and very careful and deliberate. He had the confidence of all. In personal appearance he was tall, spare, bent, lean, angular, blue-eyed, and wore blue spectacles, owing to weak eyes. He was a strong Federalist. He lived to be 100 years old. David Warner was a very large and tall man. He was a man of strong understanding, and he well knew it, and was somewhat above his contemporaries in reading, intelligence, in thought and in position. In later life his mind became unbalanced. He died nearly ninety years of age."

At what time settlements were first made in the eastern part of the town is unknown, but it is probable that they are at least as old as the settlement of Wading River. At the location called in early days the "Fresh Ponds" and now "Baiting Hollow," a settlement is believed to have been, as early as 1719, and in 1792 a church was organized with a few members. Previous to that the people had doubtless been connected with the church at Wading River, said to have been old in 1750. We may add here that the churches which were known as the "Strict Congregational," had their origin in the famous " New Light" movement that originated in New England about 1744; their leader on Long Island was Rev. Elisha Payne, who was pastor of the " New Light" church at Bridge Hampton, and whose tombstone may be seen in the Hay Ground cemetery near that village. In 1803 a small meeting house was built at Baiting Hollow, which was succeeded by the present edifice, built in 1862. Time fails us to give due justice to the memory of Rev. Manly Wells, Nathan Dickinson, David Benjamin, Azel Downs, and their successors, whose names are identified with the history of this church. The village and country round has been the home of thrifty citizens, whose family names are among the oldest in our town. It was here that the first Swedenborgian church was organized, whose leader and teacher for many years was Jonathan Horton, its chief supporter. An important item in the history of Northville is the memorable repulse of a party sent from a British squadron to capture several sloops lying near the shore, on May 31, 1814. The American militia (a small company of thirty) was under the command of Capt. John Wells, a man of resolute will and great courage, a member of the Legislature in after years, and who has left many prominent descendants, among them the late Alden Wells, a son. The attack was met with so vigorous a defense that the enemy soon withdrew, their errand unaccomplished.

Doubtless the most ancient settlement in the town is the region known as Upper and Lower Aquebogue; the latter portion being now generally known as Jamesport. From the fact that this latter region was frequently spoken of as "Old Aquebogue," we may conclude that it may claim priority of settlement, and with the more reason as it was nearer to the parent village of Southold. When these settlements were actually begun, we have at present no knowledge, but it is hoped that a more thorough investigation will eventually throw light upon the subject. From our present information, we conclude that it was about 1690. It is believed that a church was established here in the early part of the last century, and a meeting-house built on the cemetery lot, where the first interment is said to have been made in 1775. This church was doubtless an offshoot or a branch of the old church at Southold, but on the 26th of March, 1758, a "New Light" Church, or as it was called, "The First Strict Congregational Church of Southold," was organized by Rev. Elisha Payne. From the fact that they occupied the old meeting-house, we conclude that it absorbed the former organization, or at least a majority. We may say here that the "New Light" bore the same relation to the old Congregational Churches that the Puritans did to the Church of England; their motto was "Come forth from the world and be ye perfect." At intervals of a few years large numbers were added to the church by revivals of religion, and among them was Manly Wells, Daniel Youngs and David Benjamin, who, as preachers, were afterward known throughout the country. In 1797 the old church at Upper Aquebogue was replaced by a new and larger one, rebuilt in 1833, and a tall steeple, which from the peculiar nature of the country was visible for a great distance round, and gave to the building and also to the neighborhood, the name of "Steeple Church;" and this, in 1863 was replaced by a still larger building. The old one was removed to Riverhead, by the late George N. Howell, and converted into two stores, now owned by John Robert Corwin, and occupied by Davis & Son and Lee & Bunce. The names of Timothy Wells, Daniel Youngs, Moses Sweezy and Parshall Terry must ever be identified with its history. In 1829, about sixty members of this church withdrew and built a new one about half way to Riverhead, and a few years later this again was divided, part with the church building removing to Northville, the remainder to Riverhead.

The great success of Sag Harbor, as a port for whaling ships, prompted a few men, among whom the foremost were James Tuthill, of Southold, and James Halsey, of Bridge Hampton, to purchase Miamogue Neck, and establish a new seaport, which from the names of its principal founders was called Jamesport. Its rapid growth at first is mentioned by the historian Prime, who in 1845 says: "In 1833 there was not a single habitation here, now some forty." The place was well started by building a hotel and a good wharf, and at one time two or three whale ships sailed from here, but the failure of the whale fishery ended its prosperity. In 1849, James Halsey, one of the founders, started for California overland, but never reached the land of gold. The future of Jamesport is doubtless to be a summer resort, for which it is well adapted. In Lower Aquebogue, the oldest church in this town was established, it is believed as early as 1728. It was Presbyterian, and a church building was erected in 1731, and a hundred years later was repaired and enlarged. It was eventually merged into the Lower Aquebogue Congregational Church. We cannot fail to mention the Camp Meeting Association which annually in August attracts crowds of worshipers from all the country round. Jamesport will long be distinguished as the home of two brothers, Messrs. Simeon S. and Edward Hawkins, both of whom have represented the First Senatorial District at Albany, and who, belonging to different political parties, are notable illustrations of a fact which politicians sometimes forget, that men can be good representatives and not belong to your party.

A fact but little known and proper to be stated here, is that in 1793 Mrs. Phebe Wickham, at her house, near Mattituck, established the first Sunday-school in Suffolk County, only eleven years after Robert Raikes, the father of Sunday-schools, began them in London. Mrs. Wickham was a half sister of the famous traveler, John Ledyard. She died in Groton in 1840.

There are many persons besides those we have mentioned of whom extended notice should be given, like the Hon. John S. Marcy, a genial and generous man; Rev. Thomas Cook, public-spirited and of great energy; Nathan Corwin, long a leader in town matters and who in his person always seemed to us as the incarnation of Riverhead Town; his long-time partner,

John C. Davis, Member of Assembly thirty years ago; Silas S. Terry, a man greatly beloved by a wide circle of acquaintances; his partner, Joshua L. Wells, in early life a successful school teacher; Dr. R. H. Benjamin, a zealous supporter of his church and the public school, and who, as first president of the Savings Bank, laid broad and deep the foundations of its great success; his successor, Dr. A. B. Luce; John Corwin, the popular landlord; and scores of others, useful, prominent citizens of this town, who have gone to their reward; but the limit of time and space forbids; nor can we attempt to add the names of those who, natives here, have achieved honorable name elsewhere. There is one name, however, that must be mentioned. Tappin Reeve, son of Rev. Abner Reeve, a clergyman of this town, became famous as a lawyer and founder of the celebrated law school at Litchfield, Conn. He was the first eminent lawyer in this country to arraign the common law of England for its cruelty in cutting off the natural rights of married women and placing their property entirely within the control of their husbands. This year is the 100th anniversary of the passage of the first Act in our Legislature looking to the liberation of married women from this bondage, and by a law passed at our last Legislature the reform which Mr. Reeve first preached is thoroughly effected. He died in 1823, but he lived long enough to see his principles gain a footing in Connecticut, though at first they did not meet with much favor.

A book should be written to preserve the memory of what Riverhead Town did to aid in the war to preserve the Union. She promptly voted down all disloyal resolutions offered by the few sympathizers that rebellion had here, and supplied all the moneys necessary to do her part, while one hundred and twenty-two of her citizens went to the front, of whom ten never returned. Of those who did return, sixteen have answered to the last roll call here, and time is reducing the ranks of the remaining.

Then honor to the brave who nobly died;
And honor to the men who by their side
   Survived the canon's hail
   With hearts that did not quail
When all our country's fate was cast
For life or death in War's fierce blast.
—DR. WHITAKER.

The time and space we have devoted to the past forbids
our entering upon extended remarks as to the future. We
have endeavored to give a picture of the times that are
gone; but the things that are, surround us now, and they
speak for themselves. The unpainted and unsteepled meeting-house is succeeded by the elegant church edifice. The
little rustic schoolhouse of the rudest kind, and for whose
maintenance every dollar was grudged, is supplanted by the
Union School, for which no expense is too great and no orna-
ment too good. Compare the private dwelling of to-day with
the homes of our best citizens of generations past, and how
great the contrast. To-day a good selection of books and the
weekly or daily newspapers are found in every household;
then the Bible and the almanac comprised almost their only
library, and of newspapers their were none. In matters of
decoration, how great the change. There is not a house that
has not a multitude of things which the good people of the
past would have called the "superfluities of life." The
chromos and engravings that now adorn the humblest homes
would have been miracles of art a century ago. The increase
of means of communication with the outside world are too
apparent to require mention. Where the thrifty village was
in the early times we find it more thrifty still; and where once
was an unbroken forest we see around us all the evidences of
prosperity and happiness.

If towns and villages have their periods of decline it is
nothing strange, for cities and nations have the same; but the
general progress is still onward. The traveler who ascends a
lofty mountain will not find his journey one regular ascent
from the base to the summit. For a long distance he will be

38

traveling over apparently level ground; then he will ascend a slight elevation, then he will descend into a valley, and for a part of his journey he will actually be going down hill; but as he travels on he will find that the valley of the present moment is higher than the hill on which he stood an hour before. At one time he will be as completely hidden from the goal of his hopes as if he were in the center of the earth, and again he will be in full view of the object of his aspirations.

And so he goes on and on, through all changes of climate and varieties of vegetation, till he reaches that chill region of mist and cloud, where no life exists and which marks the border line of perpetual snow. But beyond all these, the cloud and darkness left behind, he enters a region of perpetual light and his feet at length tread the summit where the sun shines forever with unclouded glory.

The band here played again, and then Chairman Foster presented Prof. Joseph M. Belford of Riverhead, who delivered the following address:

What man has done, how he has done it, and what results have followed his action, are questions that not only powerfully appeal to the imagination, but engage the intellect as well. There is probably no field of investigation into which the human mind can enter that in a greater degree stimulates the curiosity, and arouses and sustains the interest, than that of human history. With unwearied patience, in the face of difficulties that seemed insurmountable, we find man feeling his way through the past, reading its cuneiform inscriptions, deciphering its Babylonian bricks, exploring its pyramids, studying its art, its architecture, its literature, anything and everything that might throw any light upon the life of a people that had played its part in the solemn drama of history.

And there is no field of study that is more fruitful of solemn lessons than this, for as man comes to study the facts of the past, not as isolated phenomena, but in their obvious and necessary relation to each other, as so many successive links in the great chain of historic evolution, he is overwhelmed with the fact that here as everywhere in the universe he is within the domain of law; that there is just as absolute and fixed an order of sequence in the phenomena of history as there is in the phenomena of nature; that the scientific observer can with no more certainty lay down the law of sequence in the facts he observes in nature, than the historical observer can lay down the law of sequence in the facts he observes in history; that things no more happen fortuitously in the growth of a nation than they happen fortuitously in the growth of a plant; that nations have a law of life and decay, just as trees have a law of life and decay; that a nation can no more grow in contravention of law than an oak can.

And whether we study the civilization of Greeks or Aztecs, of Persians or Indians, of English or French, we find the *law* of their development always the same. The reason why one nation attains a higher point of civilization than another is not that it had a *different* law of development, but that the *same* law had a freer scope and a wider range. And along broad lines these laws are very distinct. Every one, for example, recognizes that there is a necessary relation between the character of a people and their external surroundings. The student of history isn't surprised to find the Greek mind and temperament one thing, and the Asiatic mind and temperament quite another thing. The conditions of their life make this imperative. It isn't a matter of accident, it's the outworking of a fixed law. Every one of us is familiar with the *law* of supply and demand; the law of ratio between the wages of labor and the cost of food. These are things that we can't escape. They inhere in the very constitution of society. Have you ever reflected that there is a fixed ratio between the number of marriages that occur in any given year and the price of corn in that year—the higher the price of corn the fewer marriages, the lower the price of corn the more numerous the marriages? So that if the young men of Riverhead Town seriously wish to multiply their chances in this direction, let them set about lowering the price of corn.

But, seriously, when once this idea of law has possessed us, when we can see everywhere the silent, resistless play of unseen forces, working their way on and through and over all obstructions, to the final destiny which God has marked out for nature and man, " that one far-off divine event to which the whole creation moves," not only will we come to study the facts with a deepening interest, but with a deepening reverence as well, and we will come to see that history is something more than a mere catalogue of events, something more than a record of sieges and battles and crusades. We will see in it all and through it all the Divine purpose with regard to man, ever unfolding, ever ripening, through shadow and through sunshine, through the inky darkness of mediæval ignorance and the meridian splendor of Nineteenth Century knowledge, ever approaching the splendid fulfillment of which the law of development—which is stamped upon all that God has made—gives us certain assurance.

It is this conception of history that brings order out of chaos. The scientific student assures us that in the whole realm of natural phenomena there is no such thing as catastrophe; that what we are accustomed to look upon as sudden upheavals or violent cataclysms in nature, are in reality only the necessary and orderly giving way of old to new conditions under the direction of law. So, too, the historical student, from this higher standpoint of observation, assures us that there are no catastrophes in history; that amid all those social and political upheavals which threaten to disrupt society, throughout all the conventions or congresses or parliaments with their fury of debate, amid all the battle fields with their clangor of arms and their groans of the dying, always, always there has been an imperative law higher than all these things and regulating them all and evolving from them new and higher social conditions and possibilities.

Now, so much for the way in which we ought to study history. And if we are to hope for any higher or larger development in the future it must come from just such thoughtful study of the past, of the causes which contribute to its growth, of the law underlying its development. For law, my friends, can never change; it's the same for all times, all seasons, all conditions; the same for the falling apple and the blazing meteor; the same for the dew-drop and the ocean; the same for the dust molecule that noiselessly settles on your parlor mirror and the cruel avalanche thundering down the sides of the mountains; law everywhere and always the same. Conditions change, phenomena change, environment changes, but law never. So that under whatever law of life and development your ancestors lived one hundred years ago you live to-day, and you can hope for no change or advantage in this regard. It's true, the conditions of your life are widely different; it's true that your environment has been much enlarged, but be convinced of one thing, that if there was any law of relation between the means at your ancestors' command and the use they made of those means you live under the same law, and you can neither escape nor modify its operation.

Now, however complex an organization society may seem to be, yet the great principles underlying social growth are simple and obvious, and easy of statement. In the first place, man can never separate himself from nature, and it must be apparent, as I have already hinted, that very largely social development must depend on the character of our relation with the external world. Think what a wondrous storehouse this nature is. It stands for something more than a moving panorama of light and beauty, delighting the eye and feasting the imagination; something more than a treasury of wealth in precious metals and precious stones. It stands for us too as a wondrous depository of forces, ever present and always potent, from whose play we can never escape, and from a proper utilization of which it is probable there arises more substantial and permanent social development than from any other cause. I think it is not an extravagant statement to say that civilization is advanced or retarded, suffering diminishes or increases, according as man dominates or is dominated by these forces. We see him go into nature's forest, hew down her trees, transform them into dwellings, multiply these into villages, into cities, utilize her forces to do his work, to light and heat his houses, to propel his machinery, to elevate his grain, to carry his burdens, turning her to a thousand noble uses, and we cry, Behold the wondrous impetus given to the social movement! See how man is lord and master of nature! But look again. From out the summit of Vesuvius a little cloud of smoke begins to rise. The scientists watch it with interest as an evidence that other of the internal forces of nature are at work; the smoke becomes flame, the flame becomes lava and ashes; down the mountain sides it streams, burying houses, burying people; Herculaneum and Pompeii nothing more than a mighty sepulcher, entombed for hundreds of centuries. Look again. This nature denies the fruit of the earth for a season—famine comes, plague comes, and we hear the cry of anguish from starving millions in Russia or India. No, No! Any philosophy of social development that would ignore this relation of man to the world in which he lives would be singularly inadequate and incomplete. Out of this relationship spring the most magnificent discoveries of science; and along the line of scientific discovery lie some of the grandest possibilities of civilization. You don't light your houses with pine knots and tallow dips any more. Why? Because the student of nature has been abroad and has caught the lightning from the clouds and has given you it as a means of light. You no longer spend weary days jolting and bumping and exasperating yourself and your neighbor passenger in going from point to point over roads almost impassable. Why? Because scientific discovery has found in nature another mode of motion. Look where you will you find the fruits of this spirit of discovery. And as Henry Thomas Buckle says, "The discoveries of great men never leave us. They are immortal. They contain those eternal truths which survive the shock of empires, outlive the struggles of rival creeds and witness the decay of successive faiths. All these have their different measures and different standards, one set of opinions for one age, another set for another. They pass away like a dream; they are as the fabric of a vision which leave not a rack behind. The discoveries of genius alone remain. They are for all ages and all times; never young and never old, they bear the seeds of their own life. They flow on in a perennial and undying stream; they are essentially cumulative and giving birth to the additions which they subsequently receive, they thus influence the most distant posterity, and after the lapse of centuries produce more effect than they were able to do even at the moment of their promulgation."

Your ancestors of a hundred years ago hardly felt the impress of this current of discovery. But we feel it now, we are a part of it. For it is of the essence of scientific discovery that you can't limit its application as to time or place. We may say that a great deal that is going on in the scientific world is of no immediate interest or concern to us; that it can neither directly or indirectly advance or retard our development. But we're wrong if we say that. A new scientific truth is the possession of the world. It enlarges by so much our knowledge of the world in which we live, and our command of the forces by which we are surrounded. Says the same learned writer whom I have already quoted: "In a great and comprehensive view the changes in every civilized people are in their aggregate dependent on three things: First, on the amount of knowledge possessed by their ablest men; second, on the direction which that knowledge takes, that is to say, the sort of subject to which it refers; thirdly, and above all (mark that), above all on the extent to which the knowledge is diffused and the freedom with which it pervades all classes of society." And in our day, with a telegraph system girdling the earth, no sooner is a fresh scientific discovery made than it

44

becomes the possession of every race and every clime. In our age there is no such thing as a monopoly of knowledge. You may effect a corner in wheat, but you can't effect a corner in brain product. That immediately becomes the property of inquiring millions, going by so much to enrich their intellectual possessions, and so contribute to their social development. Now in the next hundred years we are to live right in the flood-tide of this tremendous impulse that has been given to scientific study and discovery. And if you will compare, and I need not make this comparison for you, the multiplied blessings which have followed these discoveries, the beneficent uses to which they have been turned—if you will compare these things with what you recollect or what you read of the conditions of life that confronted your ancestors, you may find some just basis of speculation or prophecy as to what the next hundred years may develop.

But it isn't alone in the way of outward material advantages that the spirit of scientific discovery enriches us. It does something more for us than to give us devices for lighting and heating our homes or giving us labor-saving machines. It brings within the reach of every one a literary product of which our ancestors never dreamed. I know that a great many bad books are written. I know that very much that passes under the name of poetry and romance is fit for nothing but for bonfires, and that it would make uncommonly poor material for that. I know that many of the utterances of the so-called realistic school reek with moral filth and every form of literary abomination. But I know, too, that all over the world there are intellects all aflame with the fire of genius and hearts all aglow with love to God and man, that are pouring out a stream of mental health and moral strength and spiritual beauty that must enrich the age in which they live and form a precious heritage for the future; writers whose sentiment is so pure and whose moral tone is so lofty that it finds its way as a mighty potential force into the hearts and lives of those who are aiming to make the age in which they live a better age,

45

whose aspiration is to help on the social movement along the line of loftier, purer character and an enlarged manhood and womanhood. Don't let me be misunderstood. I have no purpose to disparage the libraries of one hundred years ago. I fear we are a little too much given to patronizing our fore-fathers. We are apt to institute unfavorable comparisons between their rather limited opportunities and the almost boundless resources of the modern student. We are apt to think that they didn't have many books, and that we ought not to expect them to know very much. Well, I presume they didn't have very many books; but then I'm not sure that the value of a library is measured by the number of volumes on the shelves. There is another and a higher test than that. A book is valuable not so much for the knowledge it gives as for the character it develops. And from this higher stand-point possibly their libraries were not so meagre after all. If they had not many books they had good ones. Now and then you found Burns there—sweet, gentle Robert Burns, who has found a voice for every human sorrow, a cry to the pitying Father for every human need; whose sympathy was aroused alike by the daisy carelessly upturned by his plow and by the sorrows of struggling men and women, toiling on in obscurity under a burden of poverty. And they had their Shakespeare, to whose affluent genius all knowledge and all experience seemed an open secret; who read the human heart and un-folded its workings as astronomers read the stars and tell us their elements. And, above all and grander than all, they had their Bible, not as a text-book for critical study, but as a veri-table fountain of life, drawing from it sustenance and strength, and the amplest equipment for their daily duties. To them the songs of David meant more than the rhythm or cadence of Hebrew poetry; they meant actual power to uplift and sus-tain. To them they turned when the burden grew too heavy or the sorrow pressed too sorely, and they found in them—not words, but the Lord God himself, a tower of strength in the hour of need. And before the type of manhood and womanhood that they evolved from these elements you and I must stand to-day with uncovered heads in reverent homage. It was a manhood and womanhood that would have graced any time and any civilization. Heroic in self-sacrifice, large in charity, lofty in ideal, affluent in all the graces that adorn and dignify the human character, it ought to move you with pride to look back upon such an ancestry. In contemplation of this larger worth we lose sight of oddities of manner or extravagances of dress. These are accidental, adventitious, the creature of the hour, the whim of the moment, liable to constant change and fluctuation, but character is an undying possession, and for it we can have nothing but the deepest reverence. We may smile at the bonnet as capacious as a Saratoga trunk, or at the bodice as stiff and as unyielding as the laws of the Medes and Persians, but we don't smile at the large hearts and the generous souls which gave to Riverhead Town such a history as it has had for a hundred years.

Yet granting all this, and not losing sight for a moment of our obligation to the past, what of the future? I find it impossible to cherish the belief that the past is exhaustive of high possibilities of life and character. You may say that it is of the essence of lofty character that it be developed by hardships; that it is born in travail, nourished and perfected in suffering, and that an amelioration of the conditions of life naturally tends to an emasculation of the moral fibre, a general lowering of the moral tone. But in so saying don't you neglect another obvious arrangement in the moral economy of the universe, namely, that these very changes create new hardships, and that, however great may be the change in the condition of life, there can never be any change in the law of character? Be sure of this: God never leaves any age without the proper and necessary conditions of development. Nay, more; all history proves that He provides for an ever loftier standard of character, and places man in the very conditions which make the attainment of that standard possible. A great deal of the apprehension that is expressed for the present and for the future has its foundation in a false philosophy, and a neglect of the most obvious teachings of history. We need not fear man nor his work. Whatever obligation the future may lay upon him he will manfully meet. And this brings me to the principal purpose of my address to-day. If we look backward we see the noble line of patient men and women, working out, in the face of discouragement and difficulty, the history which is theirs and ours to-day. Their work is completed, at least so far as their active participation in it is concerned. But in the sense of there being in every good and generous deed, and in every noble life, a power of reproduction and perpetuation, that work can never die. It must form an integral part of the future history of the town by whomsoever that history shall be made. Looking forward, our eyes rest upon the youth to whom is committed the future destiny of Riverhead Town. All it is ever to become they must make it. It is an obligation that can neither be eluded nor shifted. It is an obligation that is individual and personal, it is yours and mine, and it cannot be relegated or assigned to other hands. I have hinted at the aids we are to have from the outside, in the fact that we move right along in this wonderful current of scientific discovery, of the invention of machinery, of the literary products of an age that is singularly prolific of good literary work. All these things will be ours and all will contribute to our growth. But the future history of River-head Town depends not nearly so much on what you receive from the outside, as on what you evolve from the inside; not so much on what the world gives you, as on what you give the world; not so much from the contributions you receive from the busy brain workers in the world, as on the character of the work which you produce. Now, society has a perfectly legitimate expectation of you and me, and by so much as we defect that expectation, by so much do we subtract from the possible growth and development of the town or community in which we live. The first thing that society has a right to demand of us is that we should produce something, that we should be producers and not consumers merely. That don't necessarily mean that we must produce a Paradise Lost, or an Atlantic Cable, or a Corliss engine, or a painting like the Ascension of Christ. These are among the products of genius that stand out solitary and eminent, with a yawning gulf between them and the ordinary product of the average mind. Society don't demand that we be Shakespeares, or Bacons, or Raphaels, or Edisons. It only demands, and it has a perfect right to demand, that we produce the very best of honest work of which we are capable in the sphere in which we live, and that we do that all the time. It is your work, your brain, your arm, highly consecrated and conscientiously directed to the noblest ends, that are going to give to Riverhead Town all of worth that it will develop in the next one hundred years.

Don't make the mistake of setting up a false standard or criterion by which to measure your work. Above all, don't make the mistake of supposing that your sphere of action here in Riverhead Town is necessarily limited or proscribed. It is not always those who have reached distinction in what you feel are wider spheres and by shorter roads that have the most permanently enriched the age in which they lived. And right here and now it is your opportunity to do just as noble and just as lasting work as any the world has ever seen. Do you ask me how you can do this? Now, I can give you no settled or fixed rule by which you may achieve what the world calls success, or by means of which you may be secured against the possibility of what the world calls failure. I can formulate no principles for your guidance which will certainly bring to you fame or distinction. And possibly the very worst service I could render you would be to tabulate these rules, if any such there were. But I can tell you how your life may become a potential force in the social history of Riverhead Town. It is by setting your ideal of life so high that character rather than reputation, duty rather than distinction, shall be the aim of your living. It is what we aim to do that exalts or belittles us. He

49

who lives out a noble purpose, even in obscurity, so that he lives it out truly, is the benefactor of his race. I confess to you that to me there is no more moving spectacle than to see the noble youth of our town, with a consciousness of the obligation they owe to the age in which they live, girding themselves for the life struggle before them. It partakes of the highest qualities of heroism. They are going to meet unseen dangers. They know that a thousand foes are lurking in the dark to tempt them from the high standard of life and character which they have set before them. But they are undaunted by all these things. The blood of Revolutionary sires courses in their veins. As they fought for freedom, so these will sternly strive to lay broad and deep the foundation of strong and enduring character. Like Emerson's hero, " they have not omitted the arming of the man. They have learned in season that they are born into the state of war, and that society and their own well-being require that they should not go dancing in 'the weeds of peace, but, warned, self-collected, and neither defying nor dreading the thunder, they take both reputation and life in their hands, and with perfect urbanity they dare the gibbet and the mob by the absolute truth of their speech, and the absolute rectitude of their behaviour." I am not painting an imaginary struggle. I am not dealing in rhetorical rhapsodies. I am outlining the conditions of the struggle that confronts every strong man and every earnest woman on the threshold of active life—conditions from which we can't escape, but from the right use of which the ripest fruits may be garnered and the proudest distinction gained. It is of the essence of all noble work that it carries with it its own compensation. " Work," says the seer of Concord, " in every hour, paid or unpaid; see only that thou 'work, and thou canst not escape the reward; whether thy work be fine or coarse, planting corn or writing epics, so only it be honest work, done to thine own approbation, it shall earn a reward to the senses as well as to the thought; no matter how often defeated, you are born to victory. The reward of a thing well done, is to have done it." Can you measure the moral power of the young life before me to-day, if it be so aroused and so directed? What method of calculation will you apply to the gross result of the interplay of such energies and forces in the social life of the next century?

Young man and young woman you live in an age of magnificent opportunities. Those who lived and died a hundred years ago or more, have left you a precious heritage. I don't believe the sun shines upon a land where the rewards to honest toil are so swift and so sure as here. You are barred from no honorable calling by the accident of birth or the limitation of social caste. The only coat of arms that wins genuine homage here is the shield of personal honor and personal worth. And though you be born into a state of war, girded with that shield, the issue of the conflict is never doubtful. All that the broadest minds and the stoutest hearts have done, you may do. And the one grand lesson of this day and hour is that we live up to the measure of our opportunities. The Divine purpose with regard to man is moving on, and it will be wrought out with us if we stand in the van-guard, over us if we lag behind. The lessons of the past make the prophecy of the future sure. And we can help on the dawning of this brighter day. Will we do it?

> " A sacred burden is the life ye bear;
> Look on it, lift it, bear it patiently,
> Stand up and walk beneath it steadfastly,
> Fail not for sorrow, falter not for sin,
> But onward, upward, till the goal ye win."

The benediction by Rev. Dr. Whitaker, of Southold, closed the profitable and enjoyable meeting. There were sports of various kinds at the Fair Grounds, and in the evening there was a very creditable display of fireworks set off on the south side of the river, near the water's edge, an excellent place for the purpose. The old lumber yard grounds, and vicinity opposite, were filled with a large crowd of village residents and people who had driven in to witness the show, and the expressions on all sides were that the display was one well worth seeing. At intervals, during the exhibition, the Riverhead Brass Band, from a position near Hallett's Mill, furnished inspiring strains of patriotic music, and altogether a successful and satisfactory celebration was thus fittingly brought to a brilliant close.